SWEAT

MARQUIS KINDRICK

For the heat.
For the quiet things we never say—
but live anyway.
For every city that made us hold our breath.

CHAPTER ONE — *Already Sweating*

South Los Angeles was in the middle of a heat wave.

Evening rush hour was in full effect—traffic crawling, car horns quick with attitude, the hum of box fans in every window. From the open driver's side of a Monte Carlo parked outside, the radio crackled:

"It's a hot one out there, y'all, and the heat ain't slowin' down. Ninety-eight degrees and rising…"

Inside Tarrick's apartment, the AC was on full blast, but it wasn't doing a damn thing.

Sweat ran down his body in thick trails, tracing over the abs he'd worked hard for. He was fit—lean and cut, every inch of him earned through years of discipline. Naked on the bed, one leg stretched long, the other bent at the knee, his hand moved in rhythm, chest rising fast, mouth parted.

In his mind, it wasn't his hand at all.

It was Dante.

The dream played behind his eyes like film—hot and raw. Dante's body on him, in him, heavy and urgent. Their breaths tangled, the bed creaking under the pressure of want. Dante moved like he knew exactly how Tarrick liked it, and Tarrick took it all—legs over Dante's shoulders, toes curling, slick with sweat and something more. It was perfect.

Until the doorbell rang.

The sound sliced through the room like a slap.

Tarrick jolted upright, heart pounding, hand dropping away from himself. He sat there for a beat, dazed, chest heaving. Then he scrambled off the bed, wiping himself down with the corner of a T-shirt. He yanked on a pair of gym shorts, barely registering if they were clean, and padded barefoot to the door.

He didn't check the peephole. He already knew.

When he opened it, the hallway heat hit first—thicker than inside, smelling like asphalt and someone's microwave dinner. Then came his sister, Shaunice.

She burst in like she owned the place, arms full of bags, sweat gleaming on her forehead. "Tee! You a damn angel, for real." She kissed his cheek on her way past.

Behind her was Dante.

Tarrick's breath caught.

Same face. Same thick lips. Same deep brown eyes—eyes that had just done unholy things to him in his head. But now Dante stood there in real life—thick, muscular, arms bulging beneath a white tank, full lips parted slightly as he stepped inside. Gold chain swinging with every slow stride, and also very much his sisters fiancé.

"Appreciate you lettin' us crash," Dante said, voice smooth like syrup, like he hadn't just starred in the wettest dream Tarrick had ever had five minutes ago.

Tarrick forced a nod. "Yeah… no problem."

He stepped aside, pulse still racing, and let them in.

Shaunice dropped her bags by the couch. "Plumber said it'll be at least a week before my floors dry. You sure this ain't too much?"

Tarrick shook his head. "It's cool. Y'all family. You already know where the extra room is."

Shaun smiled and disappeared down the hallway.

That left Tarrick alone with Dante.

Dante looked around, soaking in the clean space, the cool air, the view of South L.A. through the window. "Nice spot. Real clean. Smells good too."

"I keep it together," Tarrick said, trying not to stare.

"You good?" Dante asked, locking eyes with him. "You sweatin' like you ran a race."

"I was just… laying down. This heat wave ain't no joke."

Shaun's voice floated from the back. "Babe, help me with these bags."

"I see she still bossy," Tarrick said with a laugh.

Dante smirked. "She still know who's really in charge though."

Tarrick forgot to breathe for a second as Dante turned and walked down the hall.

That body, that voice, that walk—

Tarrick knew he should've been working on his manuscript, finishing his next book, but the heat—and the thought of Dante—had other plans.

This was going to be a problem.

CHAPTER TWO — *One Week*

The sun dipped low across South L.A., casting the buildings in gold and the streets in soft, melting pastels. The heat still hung in the air—heavy and wet, clinging to skin like a second layer. The kind of heat that made you move slower, talk lighter, or risk sweating through your clothes just standing still.

Tarrick leaned on the patio fence, a glass of red wine in his hand, glancing up at his own apartment above. Down here at his friends place, the soft hum of a jazz playlist drifted from inside the house—low enough not to overpower the evening, smooth enough to match it.

AJ and José were posted up on the chic patio set, both with glasses in hand and shirts barely buttoned.

AJ, beautiful as ever—dark chocolate skin, sharp cheekbones, thick arms peeking from a loose tank—tilted his wine toward the sidewalk.

"I saw somebody fine as hell goin' into your apartment earlier," he said, a teasing grin on his lips.

Tarrick raised an eyebrow. "What about the girl walking in right in front of him? You casually missed her?"

AJ chuckled. "I clocked her. But I was focused."

"That girl is my sister."

AJ winced playfully. "Damn."

They all laughed.

"Pipes burst in her place," Tarrick said, swirling the wine in his glass. "Flooded the whole downstairs. I'm letting her and her man stay here while they get it fixed."

AJ raised an eyebrow. "That fine man is her man?"

"Yup," Tarrick said flatly. "And I know y'all got your open arrangement or whatever—but Dante is off limits."

AJ leaned back in his chair, smirking. "Aren't they all… until they're not?"

José smiled but stayed quiet, sipping his wine with that calm, watchful energy.

"I'm serious," Tarrick said, eyes sliding between them. "Behave. They're here for a week. He's more than a man, they're engaged."

José stretched out his legs. "If Ezekial would finally fix that damn pool, maybe we all could actually cool off. This heat is disrespectful."

They glance at the covered pool in the center of the entire apartment complex like a resort no one could enjoy.

"And rent too damn high for broken amenities," AJ added.

They all murmured in agreement.

AJ raised his glass. "To fixing busted shit and surviving the week."

Tarrick clinked his glass against theirs.

"Surviving the week," he echoed, trying to keep his tone light. But the words felt heavier than they should've.

He took a slow sip, eyes drifting back up to his apartment.

One week.
He just had to make it one week.

CHAPTER THREE — *Steam*

By the time Tarrick got back upstairs from AJ and José's, night had fully fallen over South L.A. The air outside had cooled slightly, but inside, the apartment still clung to the day's heat like sweat on skin.

The place wasn't messy, just... different now. Lived in. Like it belonged to more than one person. A cereal box sat on the counter instead of on top of the fridge with the rest, and that small thing annoyed him more than it should've. He picked it up and returned it to its place, letting his fingers rest on the fridge for a second before his phone buzzed.

His sister, Shaunice.

He answered on speaker. "Yo."

"I'm just gettin' off work," she said. "You want anything from Church's?"

"They still got those honey butter biscuits?"

"Boy, you know they do."

"Then yeah. Gimme one."

"Ask Dante what he wants too. He not answering his phone."

Tarrick hesitated. "I'll find him. I'll text you his order."

"Bet. Byeeeee."

"Byyyyyye."

The call ended with their usual sing-song, playful and soft.

Tarrick pocketed his phone and headed down the hall.

"Dante?" he called out. Nothing.

The door to the guest room was half open. He pushed it gently.

The bedroom was dim, empty, quiet except for the low hiss of water running. The bathroom door inside was wide open, and steam was pouring out thick and steady.

Tarrick stepped in.

The mirror over the vanity gave him a perfect view.

Dante stood under the spray in the glass-walled shower, naked and glistening. Water streamed down his back, over his broad chest, across carved abs. His skin gleamed. Muscles flexed. One hand moved slowly between his legs, soap sliding down the length of his dick—thick, long, impossible to ignore.

Tarrick's throat dried up. His heart thudded against his ribs. His hand dropped to his waistband before he even knew what he was doing, palm pressing over the hardness that had grown quick and heavy.

He couldn't look away.

The steam curled around him like a hand, and his mind blurred with it.

In the dream, he was in the shower too. Pressed up close, the water running hot between them, skin to skin. Dante reached for his hand, guided it down, wrapped it around his own length.

"That what you want?" Dante asked, low in his ear.

Tarrick's voice came out broken. "It's what I need."

Dante kissed him—soft, slow, like they had time. Then again, deeper, wetter, harder.

Their bodies pulsed against each other. Dicks hard, chests slick, lips locked. Dante's mouth found his neck, tongue trailing heat down to his collarbone.

Then he turned Tarrick around, big hands gripping his hips.

"Yes, Daddy," Tarrick whispered, chest pressed to glass, legs weak with want.

The water shut off.

Tarrick jerked out of the dream like waking from a fall. He backed away from the doorway, chest tight, eyes wide.

Through the steam, he saw Dante reach for a towel.
He slid the shower door open, water dripping from every inch of him, steam rising like smoke as he stepped out.

Tarrick turned and slipped out of the room fast, heart hammering.

Inside, Dante paused, towel wrapped low on his hips.
He glanced toward the mirror. Thought he heard something. Movement, maybe. A breath.

But the bedroom behind him was still.

Empty.

The air, though...
Something about it felt touched.

CHAPTER FOUR — *Creative Juices*

The morning sun poured through the blinds, bold and bright, dragging Tarrick out of sleep like a rude joke. He groaned, rubbed his eyes, and shuffled barefoot into the kitchen.

Shaunice stood at the stove in her scrubs, flipping eggs with one hand, phone in the other. The smell of butter and heat filled the space.

"Mmm," Tarrick said, leaning in the doorway. "It smells good in here. What you makin' us?"

Shaunice tossed him a look over her shoulder. "Us? Boy, this is for me. Quick breakfast before work."

Tarrick frowned and opened the fridge. "That was the last of the eggs…"

"I'll pick up more after my shift." She shrugged. "Don't catch an attitude over two damn eggs."

"You at least get my honey butter biscuit?"

Shaunice smirked. "You were knocked out when I got home. I ate that too."

Tarrick rolled his eyes and let the fridge door swing shut harder than it needed to.

Shaunice wiped her hands on a paper towel, shifting tones. "I'm really startin' to get fed up with Dante. Still ain't found a job."

Tarrick straightened, catching himself. "He says he's trying."

He heard the softness in his own voice and quickly added, "But yeah. Nah. He needs to try harder."

"Exactly." She wrapped her sandwich in a napkin and snatched her keys off the counter. "He better figure it out quick. 'Cause if he don't, when I move back in, he's not."

And just like that, she was out the door.

Tarrick exhaled and turned to the sink. He ran hot water, added a few pumps of dish soap, and dunked in the skillet from the stove. The bubbles rose up like fog, and for a second he just stared into them, mind nowhere good.

Then came footsteps.

Tarrick looked up—and nearly dropped the pan.

Dante walked into the kitchen in nothing but boxers, the button undone. Skin golden in the sunlight. Abs tight. That same gold chain swinging low on his chest like punctuation.

"Damn," Dante muttered. "It's hot as fuck."

Tarrick forced his eyes back to the sink. "Yeah. Tell me about it."

Dante leaned against the fridge, sweat already starting to gather at his temples. He opened the fridge looking for water.

"I heard y'all talkin' earlier."

Tarrick tensed. "Yeah?"

"I know I gotta get on it," Dante said. His voice wasn't defensive, just worn. "It's hard out here with a record. They look at your past before they look at your name."

Tarrick dried the skillet with slow, deliberate movements. "You'll find something. Just gotta keep pushing."

His eyes flicked down—just for a second.

That undone button.

A sliver of skin.

A glimpse of something he shouldn't want.

He gripped the skillet tighter.

I could drop right here, he thought. Pull it out the slit, take it in my mouth, feel it swell—

"Tarrick?"

His head snapped up.

"You good?" Dante asked, brow lifted.

"Yeah," Tarrick said quickly. He shoved the skillet into the cabinet and shut the door. "Just... zoned out."

Dante chuckled. "I should get on your hustle, that entrepreneur shit."

Tarrick gave a half-smile.

"When's your next book dropping?" Dante asked.

"Been stuck lately. Writer's block." He shrugged. "Guess I need new inspiration."

Dante tilted his head. "Let me know what I can do to help get your creative juices flowing."

Then he turned and walked out, chain catching the light, hips loose, confidence easy.

Tarrick watched him go.

Then fainted.

Not metaphorically.

Collapsed, lightheaded, dropping to the ground with a thud.

CHAPTER FIVE — *No Exertion*

Tarrick came to under fluorescent lights, flat on his back in a gown that left his whole ass out.

"What the hell...?"

The sheets itched. The AC blew too cold. And there, slouched in the chair beside him, was Dante.

"You passed out," Dante said, scrolling casually through his phone. "Heat exhaustion. Scared the hell outta me."

Tarrick groaned. "You serious? I really needed to come to the hospital for that?"

Dante shrugged. "I mean, you hit the floor like somebody unplugged you. Better safe than sorry."

Just then, the nurse stepped in—older Black woman, no-nonsense face, soft voice. She carried a clipboard like it was gospel.

"Good, you're awake," she said, glancing at his chart. "We ran fluids, electrolytes, gave you something for the headache. You need to stay hydrated, especially in this heat. That Los Angeles sun is no joke right now."

"Yes, ma'am," Tarrick said, sheepish.

"You're good to go once you feel steady on your feet. No heavy exertion for a day or two. Got it?"

Tarrick nodded, trying not to smirk at the irony. No exertion. Too late for that.

She offered a knowing smile—like she'd seen this exact foolishness before—and walked out, shoes squeaking.

Dante stood and opened the cabinet, pulling out the folded clothes. "You good to change by yourself, or you need me to help with your drawers?"

Tarrick gave him a look. "I'm good."

Dante laughed. "Alright. I'll step out and give you a minute."

"Thanks," Tarrick said, watching him walk away.

Stopping at the door. "Shaunice is on her way, you know she work right upstairs on the second floor," Dante reminded, before letting the door click shut behind him.

Tarrick exhaled and let his head fall back against the pillow. This whole day had spiraled—from thirst trap to actual collapse.

One more reason to keep it together, he thought, sitting up slowly. Because if Dante finds out what really had me breathless...

Yeah.

He'd never live that down.

CHAPTER SIX — *Edges*

The evening in South L.A. was muggy—still and heavy like the air itself was holding its breath. Buzz had been circulating for months about *Somerville*, the restaurant filmmaker Issa Rae opened in the neighborhood. Not just because of her name, but because of what the place was: elegant, unapologetically Black, rooted in nostalgia and draped in velvet. South Central had never seen anything quite like it.

Outside, the streetlamps started to glow, as Tarrick, Shaunice, and Dante strolled past them—dressed like they had reservations and something to prove.

Dante gave Tarrick a once-over as they neared the entrance. "You clean up nice."

Shaunice tossed her curls and added, "Please. My brother been sharp."

Tarrick grinned. "Y'all ain't lookin' too bad yourselves."

They stepped into Somerville and were greeted by the low hum of jazz and the scent of saffron and smoked butter. Inside, the restaurant felt like a dream someone had about Black L.A. in the '40s—before time and budget cuts got in the way.

Shaunice glanced around with a low whistle. "It's bougie up in here," she muttered, like being impressed might cost her something.

Tarrick smirked. "You only sent me, what—four TikToks? Talkin' about how bad you wanted to come."

She laughed, adjusting her dress as they were led to their table.

Their server arrived with chilled cucumber water and gave the rundown of the evening's specials. The room was warm with chatter, low lighting, linen napkins folded sharp.

The server left to give them a moment.

"I don't like that you're paying for everybody," Dante said, eyes still locked on the menu.

Tarrick didn't look up. "You saved my life earlier. Let me do this."

Shaunice rolled her eyes and cut in, voice just sharp enough to slice. "Maybe if you got a damn job, you'd be the one treating us."

The words hit the table like a dropped knife.

Dante stiffened. His jaw locked. His thumb started rubbing the edge of his menu like it was an escape hatch.

Tarrick's voice dropped. "Shaunice. Not tonight."

She held his gaze for a second longer, then took a slow sip of her cucumber water like it was tequila.

"I'm just sayin'," she muttered.

The silence that followed was slick with tension. The jazz kept playing, soft and pretty, completely unbothered.

"Let's just enjoy dinner," Tarrick said. "Nobody faint. Nobody fight."

Shaunice snorted. A half-laugh, half-warning shot.

Dante cracked his knuckles under the table. "Cool."

Their server returned to take their order. And though no one said it aloud, they all felt the same thing: this night had edges—but it wasn't over yet.

Later that night, after bellies were full, dessert devoured, and the ride home passed in tight-lipped silence, one thing was certain:

The food had been great.

But maybe not them.

Tarrick lay flat on his back, sheets tangled at his waist, the ceiling fan slicing slow, lazy circles above. The air was still too warm. His thoughts were worse.

He needed water.

He swung his legs over the bed and padded barefoot into the kitchen in just his briefs. The apartment was dim, moonlight slanting through the blinds in clean strips. He cracked open the fridge, grabbed a bottle, and turned—

Startled.

Dante was on the couch, half-sitting under a thin blanket, eyes just catching the light.

"Damn," Tarrick exhaled, clutching the water. "You scared the hell outta me."

Dante sat up slightly. "My bad, bro. Didn't mean to. Shaun kicked me out the room."

Tarrick blinked. "Wait—what?"

"She's still pissed," Dante said with a tired shrug. "About the job thing. Me not pullin' my weight."

Tarrick took a long drink, eyes still adjusting. "Damn. She really that mad?"

Dante nodded, rubbing the back of his neck. "Yeah. I mean… I get it. Tomorrow I'm just gon' start doing Lyft. Run a few rides across the city 'til I hear back from someone."

Tarrick leaned against the counter, bottle in hand. "That's smart."

There was a pause, thick with something unspoken.

"By the way," Dante said, voice quieter now, "thank you. For dinner. That meant a lot."

Tarrick hadn't expected that. Not the softness in the words. Not from him.

"Yeah," he said. "Of course."

Dante leaned back again, blanket slipping down his bare chest. His eyes closed, and for the first time that day, he looked peaceful. Like maybe sleep might actually come.

"You get some rest, alright?" Dante murmured without looking.

Tarrick lingered a moment too long, the cold bottle dripping slightly in his hand.

"You too," he said quietly. "And... if you ever need to talk or whatever—just knock."

Dante didn't open his eyes, but the corner of his mouth lifted in something close to a smile.

"Appreciate you."

Tarrick turned and headed down the hall, his bare feet silent on the wood.

But sleep wouldn't come easy—not with that image burned into his mind:

Dante, quiet on the couch, bare chested, full of thank-you's, wrapped in a kind of vulnerability you didn't see from him often.

Maybe ever.

And just like that, Tarrick's thirst was back—though this time, water wasn't gonna fix it.

CHAPTER SEVEN — *Caught*

The next day, Tarrick had the apartment to himself.

Shaunice was at work. Dante had left to do Lyft. It had been a while since the space felt quiet—still. A pause in the noise.

He opened his laptop and stared at the blank page.

Finally, he had a moment to write.

Finally, he had something to write about.

He started typing, fingers finding rhythm, thoughts spilling faster than he could catch them. The story poured out—new characters, a new setting—but he knew what it really was. Knew who the characters were modeled after.

Knew who he was imagining.

It was a laundromat—

Late at night. The rain poured hard, really hard. Banging against the window from heavy winds. Thunder growling overhead. Lightning flashing through the front windows in sharp, jagged bursts. Tarrick fed wet clothes into the dryer, trying not to flinch at the noise outside.

Then—

The bell above the door jingled. Dante stepped in, soaked from head to toe. Drenched like he'd walked through a hurricane. Tarrick looked up, heart hammering in his chest. "You good?"

Dante ran a hand across his face, water dripping down his jaw. "Rain came outta nowhere."

"Yeah," Tarrick said softly. "Come here. Let's get you dried off."

He reached for Dante's shirt, peeling the wet fabric up and over thick shoulders, fingers brushing hot skin underneath. Dante's abs glistened under the fluorescent lights. Tarrick dropped the shirt on a nearby bench.

"Let's get you out of these pants too," Tarrick said.

Dante raised an eyebrow. "You really gonna take care of me?"

Tarrick knelt in front of him, eyes never leaving his. "With pleasure."

His hands moved to the fly, unzipping slowly, then unbuttoning. The jeans dropped to Dante's ankles with a heavy wet slap.

He reached through the slit of Dante's boxers—fingers slow, deliberate—and pulled him out.

Long. Heavy. A memory from the day he watched him in the shower.

Tarrick licked his lips. Then leaned in.

Back in the real world, Tarrick's head tipped back against his chair, eyes fluttering shut, breath shallow. One hand stayed on the keyboard. The other worked between his legs, stroking fast and hungry. He rolled away from the desk, legs spread wide, chest rising and falling like he'd just run a mile.

Then—

"Shit!"

The voice startled him.

His eyes flew open just in time to see Dante—the real Dante—standing in the doorway, wide-eyed.

They locked eyes for a second too long.

Dante's gaze dropped. His expression unreadable.

"Damn. My bad." His voice was tight.

He turned and walked out, door shutting behind him with a heavy click.

Tarrick sat frozen, heat rising up his neck like fire. Shame punched through his chest.

Fuck.

He yanked up his sweats, wiped his hand, and stared at the document still glowing on his laptop.

Fantasy was safe.

Reality? That was dangerous.

CHAPTER EIGHT — *Wet*

The pool—centerpiece of the complex—was finally fixed, and just like that, the whole place came alive.

Children shrieked from the shallow end, their splashes echoing. An older woman bobbed on a neon floatie, sipping something from a solo cup. Chris Brown's *"Pills & Automobiles"* bumped from a speaker perched on a towel-covered chair—bass-heavy, summer-slick, pure temptation—and somebody had the grill going, sending smoke curling into the heavy air. Coconut oil, hot links, and chlorine mingled in the breeze like a scent memory from a Black childhood.

For the first time in what felt like forever, it wasn't just hot—it was a vibe.

Tarrick walked out onto the concrete in tight red trunks, a towel slung across his shoulders like a shield. His chest was bare, abs on point, but his face gave him away—tight-lipped, annoyed, distracted. A couple neighbors nodded his way; he didn't return it.

AJ spotted him first from where he and José sat near the pool steps, feet submerged.

"Damn," AJ said, tilting his shades down. "What's wrong with you?"

José leaned forward, grinning. "Oop—he got that 'don't ask' energy. This feels like tea."

Chris Brown's hook drifted louder from the speaker. Tarrick slid his feet into the pool and muttered, "Breezy should've just called this song Wet."

AJ snorted. "Right? Like—Pills & Automobiles? Be serious."

Tarrick tossed his towel onto a nearby chair, the cool bite of the water crawling up his calves like relief and restraint.

"Ain't no tea," Tarrick muttered finally. "Just this heat got me miserable."

AJ nodded toward the apartment building. "How's your guests?"

Tarrick didn't answer right away. His jaw flexed. He swirled his feet in the water, watching ripples instead of friends.

"I'm just surprised Ezekiel, the property manager, actually fixed the pool," he said finally.

They all glanced up as the screen door clacked open above them.

Dante.

He stepped out in black trunks, no shirt, no towel, just skin and confidence. His body looked dipped in gold under the sun —broad chest, abs carved, and thighs thick.

His walk was casual, unbothered—but he looked straight at them.

All three turned away immediately.

AJ was the first to speak. "I brought wine."

Tarrick blinked. "You always got wine."

AJ, with a sly smirk, "In the words of our dear Ru—if you stay ready, you ain't got to get ready."

Tarrick snorted. "That part."

AJ poured, careful not to spill. José handed Tarrick a glass.

Tarrick sipped, his shoulders easing slightly—but his eyes flicked back to Dante.

Dante hadn't joined them. He was by the grill now, joking with someone, but his back was turned just enough to keep them curious. The curve of his spine, the flex of his arms as he flipped something on the grill, the occasional glance over his shoulder—

It was nothing.

It was everything.

Tarrick told himself he was reading into it. Into everything. Told himself last night didn't mean anything on the couch. That Dante walking in on him earlier—on that—was just bad timing, a mistake, a weird blip.

But his body hadn't forgotten.

Neither had Dante's eyes, it seemed.

AJ leaned in a little. "You know he saw you, right?"

Tarrick's head whipped around. "What?"

"Earlier," AJ said. "When he came out. He looked dead at you before y'all turned your heads like synchronized swimmers."

José chuckled softly.

Tarrick rolled his eyes, but it wasn't denial. It was defense.

He drained his glass.

The wine was cold. His skin was hot. And though the pool was cool, inside, he was still sweating.

CHAPTER NINE- *What's Cooking*

Tarrick stepped into the apartment, skin still damp from the pool, towel draped over his shoulders. The cool indoor air clashed with the lingering heat of the concrete, but what really hit was the smell.

Fried chicken. Potatoes and onions. Grease, garlic, comfort.

The kitchen was alive—oil snapping in the deep fryer, the skillet hissing with every flip Shaunice made of the potatoes. Her hair tied up in a loose wrap, her scrubs half-buttoned, face glowing from the stove heat.

Tarrick grinned. "Damn. Smells like Grandma's in here."

Shaunice didn't turn. "You already know. Got it from her. Mama couldn't fry chicken if Jesus himself seasoned it first."

He laughed, dragging his towel off and tossing it over a chair. "Facts."

She smiled, but didn't look away from the stove.

"I'm gonna shower real quick," he said, already heading down the hall.

"Tee."

He stopped, turned. "Yeah?"

She was still at the stove, spatula in one hand, voice lower now. "You think I'm too hard on Dante?"

The question hung in the air, heavier than the oil smoke.

Tarrick walked back toward the kitchen, leaning against the counter, his skin still glistening. "I think... it's tough out here for people with records. Especially Black men. Even when they've changed."

Shaunice's jaw tightened. "They got him for possession with intent to distribute. Just because it was bagged up. No money, no weapon, no nothing. He had it on him, yeah—but that charge made it sound like he was running a whole operation."

Tarrick blinked. "That'll stick."

"Exactly," she said. "And he don't even do that anymore. Hasn't in a long time. But try applying for jobs with that on your record. They don't care about context."

He nodded slowly. "A felony follows you. Even after you've stopped being the person who caught it."

Shaunice flipped the potatoes, turning golden, scent heavenly, and turned off the burner. "I love him. I do. But I'm tired. Of carrying all this. Rent. Groceries. His pride. Everything."

"You ever tell him that?"

She glanced at him. "Every damn day. He hears me. But hearing ain't the same as listening."

They stood in it for a second—kitchen thick with heat, oil, silence.

"He says he's trying," Tarrick said finally. "From what I've seen... I think he is."

She wiped her hands on a towel, resting them on her hips. "Trying don't stretch my paycheck. Trying don't fix the fact that I had to ask my little brother to let us stay here in the first place."

Tarrick didn't argue. Just nodded.

Then, her voice softened. "I just want something to shift."

Tarrick gave her a half-smile. "Maybe it already is."

Shaunice sighed and turned back to the counter. "Hurry up, foods almost done."

He raised his hands in surrender. "Yes, ma'am," making his way to his room.

CHAPTER TEN — *Daddy*

Tarrick woke to the sound of grunts in the living room, sun blazing through the blinds. At first, he thought it was a dream—low, rhythmic sounds that made his heart race for reasons beyond sleep.

He pushed out of bed and cracked his door.

There, in the middle of the living room, Dante was shirtless doing push-ups, muscles flexing, sweat glistening on his back in the golden morning light. The chain around his neck swung with each rep.

Tarrick's breath caught.

He started to close the door. He wasn't ready. Not to talk about *what happened.* Not to relive the look on Dante's face when he walked in on him yesterday—dick in hand, fantasy mid-bloom. Maybe he'd just hide until they went back to their place in a few days.

But just as the door was about to shut, Dante's voice called out.

"Wait."

Tarrick paused, hand on the doorframe. Shit.

He turned, casual as if he could fake it. "What's up?"

Dante pushed up off the floor, breathing a little heavy. "Can you talk to your sister for me? See if she'll let me sleep in the bed again? My back is killin' me from that couch."

Tarrick scratched his head. "I actually talked to her last night. Thought she was gonna let you back in."

"With any luck, tonight," Dante said. "Maybe she needed time to sleep on it."

"She gone already?"

"Yeah. About thirty minutes ago."

"Oh. Cool." Tarrick started to turn again, hoping that was it.

But Dante spoke once more.

"Hey… she said you're good with massages."

Tarrick froze.

"I could use one. If you don't mind."

A pause. A long one.

"Yeah," Tarrick said, voice steady but breath caught. "Yeah, come on."

He stepped back, letting Dante follow him into the room.

Dante sat on the edge of Tarrick's bed, his wide back rising and falling. Tarrick climbed up behind him, straddling his hips as his hands found those broad shoulders.

The first touch sent a jolt through him. Heat bloomed beneath his skin.

"So," Tarrick managed, working his fingers into the knots beneath Dante's neck, "how's the Lyft thing going?"

"Interesting," Dante said, his voice low. "L.A.'s full of characters. I did have this cool white couple though, had me take them to Malibu from LAX. Tipped big too. But that airport traffic? Hell."

They chuckled softly.

"Damn," Dante said after a beat, "that feels good."

Tarrick smiled. "Happy to help."

They caught each other's reflection in the mirror across the room—Tarrick behind him, hands working, chest bare. Their eyes locked.

Dante looked away first.

"So how's the new book coming?" he asked, voice slightly hoarse. "Another bestseller in the making?"

"I hope so," Tarrick said, focusing on a knot in Dante's back. "I've got good inspiration lately."

Dante groaned again as Tarrick's thumb dug deeper. "Fuck… you got magic hands."

Then, softly: "Let me get you now."

Tarrick hesitated. "I'm good."

"Nah, c'mon," Dante said, standing. "I got hands myself."

Tarrick agreed before he could think twice. He lay on his stomach, trying to hide the semi rising in his shorts.

Dante climbed over him, straddling him, his warm hands beginning to knead into Tarrick's lower back. The weight of him. The way he settled in. The feel of his thighs against Tarrick's sides.

"So," Dante murmured, "about your book. You think it's gold?"

"I think so," Tarrick said, voice muffled by the sheets.

Dante worked deeper. Tarrick's body melted under his touch. His eyes fluttered shut.

"I've got real inspiration now," he added. "Somebody's got my juices flowing."

Dante paused—just a beat.

"Is that right."

Then he kept going, hands slower now, firmer.

Tarrick felt it.

Dante's dick, hardening between them. Pressing into the curve of his ass through the thin layer of fabric.

It was impossible to ignore.

Tarrick lifted himself up slightly, turning just enough to meet Dante's gaze.

"You okay?" Dante asked, breath shallow.

Tarrick didn't answer.

He just kissed him.

Their lips crashed. First soft. Then urgent. Hungry.

Tarrick flipped him over onto the bed, straddling him, kissing deeper—tongues tangling, hands everywhere. He reached down and cupped Dante through his mesh shorts, feeling the heat, the size, the way it jumped beneath his palm.

He kissed down Dante's chest—slow, wet kisses tracing over abs, lingering at the waistband.

Then he mouthed over the bulge, lips teasing the shape through mesh.

Dante exhaled hard. "Fuck…"

Tarrick reached in and pulled him out—thick, warm, bricked, already leaking.

"Wait," Dante said suddenly. "What about Shaun?"

Tarrick looked up at him… then back at the dick in his hand.

He didn't answer.

He opened his mouth and took Dante deep.

Dante's head dropped back, a loud groan tearing from his throat. Finally, not a dream, a very real reality.

"Close the door," Dante said, breathless.

Tarrick scrambled up, shut and locked it, then stripped completely. His dick slapped against his stomach as he returned to the bed.

He dropped to his knees between Dante's legs, took him back in —lips wrapped tight, sucking slow and deep, the room hot with breath and sweat. His hand gripped the base as his mouth worked the tip, tongue circling, teasing.

Dante grabbed a handful of Tarrick's ass. "Damn… I didn't know all that was underneath them shorts."

Tarrick came up for air, lips slick, smirking. "You weren't looking hard enough."

Then Dante flipped him—fast—his mouth finding Tarrick's ass, tongue diving in. Wet. Deep. Greedy.

Tarrick groaned, gripping the sheets, hips rising into every stroke. Years of fantasy now unfolding, and it was better than he imagined.

Dante rose behind him, spit slicking his dick.

Tarrick reached over, breathless. "Lube's in the drawer."

Dante found it. Squirted it out, coating himself until he shined. He slid a hand between Tarrick's cheeks, fingers spreading him.

Tarrick kissed Dante once more, tasting himself on Dante's lips, then helped guide the head to the spot.

Dante pushed in—slow, deliberate.

Tarrick gasped, his body stretching, aching, opening.

"You good?" Dante asked, voice ragged.

Tarrick looked back over his shoulder, eyes glazed.

"Yes, Daddy… fuck me."

Dante did just that.

His hips began to move, each thrust harder, deeper, the bed creaking beneath them. Skin slapping, breaths syncing. Tarrick moaned into the mattress, loving the weight of him, the power, the rhythm.

Dante grunted, grabbing his waist, pulling him back into each stroke.

Tarrick's eyes rolled. He couldn't think. Could barely breathe.

Dante fucked him like he meant it. Like he'd wanted it. Like he'd dreamed about it too.

Then—his voice low, strained, right in Tarrick's ear:

"I'm gonna cum…"

"Do it," Tarrick whispered. "Cum in me."

Dante's thrusts sped up—sloppy, desperate. Then his whole body seized.

A deep, guttural moan ripped from his chest as he came hard inside Tarrick, pulsing deep, filling him up, hips jerking with every wave.

Tarrick collapsed fully into the sheets, Dante still inside him, both of them breathless, soaked in sweat and silence.

For a moment, nothing moved.

Then Dante rested his head against Tarrick's back.

They didn't say another word.

But everything had changed.

CHAPTER ELEVEN — *Clarity*

The sun eased down over South L.A., casting long shadows across the hardwood floors. The sky outside the window was burnt orange, fading into plum. The heat hadn't let up, but the light had—softened now, like the city was finally exhaling.

Tarrick sat at his desk, shirtless, fingers gliding across the keyboard. The hum of his box fan battled with the clack of each key as he typed.

Two people. Both carrying weight they hadn't admitted. Both burning in silence, pretending they didn't feel it.
But they did.
And when the moment came, they gave in.
Not out of weakness, but need.
Desire, for once, didn't feel wrong. It felt right. Necessary.
Inevitable.

He paused, staring at the screen. His pulse wasn't racing this time. There was no guilt, no fear—just clarity. A stillness. He knew this story now.

For hours, the words had poured out of him. Scene after scene. Touch after touch. He hadn't written like this in months.

Inspiration didn't just strike—it landed like lightning. And its name was *Dante.*

Tarrick leaned back in his chair, letting the weight of the day settle. The air was thick, the scent of reheated fried chicken still hanging faintly in the room, mixing with the tang of sweat and the trace of body wash that lingered from his bathroom, where both he and Dante had showered together away the smell of sex.

He saved the document, fingers hovering over the title line.

He thought about the heat. The tension. The need.

Then, slowly, he typed: **SWEAT**

He hit save.

The screen dimmed slightly as his laptop went quiet.

Tarrick exhaled and rose from his seat, the sun's final rays slipping away behind him.

Tonight, there was nothing more to say.

The story—at least on the page—was finally breathing on its own.

CHAPTER TWELVE — *Focus*

The next morning, the heat hadn't fully kicked in yet, but Tarrick's room was already warm—sunlight pouring through the blinds in tight white lines across his bare chest. He was hunched over his laptop, deep in the world of SWEAT. The words flowed easy now —fantasies blurred into fiction, every scene more daring, more reckless.

On the screen, his two main characters were tangled together in the back seat of a rideshare, fog on the windows, hips rocking, sweat dripping down chests slick with—

Knock knock.

Tarrick blinked, startled. He rolled his desk chair backward and swiveled lazily toward the door. Instead of getting up, he just reached over and cracked it open.

Shaunice stood there in her scrubs, hair wrapped, brows lifted.

"Shaun? You still here?"

"Yeah," she said, pushing the door open more. "Called the office. Told 'em I'd be late."

Tarrick sat up a little straighter. Something in her voice.

"I need to talk to you," she said, stepping into the room.

He froze. Was the cat out?

"Okay... what's up?"

Shaunice crossed her arms, looking him dead in the face. "What's going on with Dante?"

Tarrick blinked, keeping his face still. "What do you mean?"

"I mean," she said slowly, "I let him back in the bed last night. Thought maybe we could reconnect… but he knocked straight out. Woke up this morning and he was already gone doing Lyft."

Tarrick nodded carefully, waiting for the punchline.

"We haven't had sex in over a week," she said. "I thought it was just because we were mad at each other. Or because he was on that damn couch."

She stared at him now. Unblinking.

"But now he's back in the bed… and he still doesn't touch me?"

Tarrick's throat tightened. "Maybe… maybe he doesn't wanna have sex in your brother's house?"

Shaunice scoffed. "Since when does Dante care about that? You think we've never done it in someone else's apartment before?"

Tarrick shrugged. "I'm just saying— wait, have y'all done it here before?"

"Focus— if he's not getting it from me," she said, her voice rising, "he's getting it from somebody. I don't like this rideshare shit. How do I know he's actually driving? Or who he's really picking up? What if he's seeing someone else? Hooking up with his damn passengers?"

Tarrick stood, voice calm. "Shaun, breathe. I highly doubt Dante is sleeping with his passengers."

She narrowed her eyes at him. "You sound real sure."

"I just don't think he's that type," Tarrick said quickly. "You know him."

Shaunice paced the room once, then pointed toward the door. "Well I'm about to get to the bottom of it. And whoever this heffa is that thinks she can sleep with my man?" She snapped her fingers. "She better be ready to get dealt with."

She stormed out, keys jangling, scrubs flaring behind her.

Tarrick stood there in the doorway, blinking, mouth slightly open.

"Oh my God," he whispered to himself.

"What the hell have I gotten myself into?"

CHAPTER THIRTEEN — *Keep it Clean*

The iconic Hollywood sign loomed in the distance, high above the haze, watching as tourists swarmed the Walk of Fame below—snapping photos at the Chinese Theatre, crowding Ripley's Believe It or Not, lining up at the wax museum like fame could rub off just by standing close.

Inside the cool, sleek lobby of the BWE Media Networks building, everything smelled like air conditioning and money. The floors gleamed, the glass shimmered, and Tarrick stepped off the elevator looking clean—jaw sharp, fresh line up, and suited up. Too hot for all that? Absolutely. But this was corporate world. Image mattered.

"Nia," he said, flashing a grin.

The receptionist looked up and lit up. "Tarrick! Come here."

They hugged briefly. She looked immaculate, her locs freshly done down her back.

"Mr. Burch is wrapping a call," she said. "Shouldn't be long."

Tarrick stood in the lobby, eyes drifting across the wall of accolades. Framed bestsellers. National Book Award shortlists. Covers of polished Young Adult novels the company had shepherded to market—including his own.

He felt the weight of it all. The shelf. The legacy. The unspoken message: **Keep it clean. Keep it safe.**

But *this* book? This one was different.

"So," Nia said from behind the desk, eyeing him with a smirk. "Can I get a preview of the new one? You doing a part two to your last hit?"

Tarrick chuckled, loosening his collar just slightly. "Actually… this one's kind of raunchy."

Nia blinked. "*Raunchy?* From you?"

He shrugged. "I've got stories to tell. Not all of them fit in one lane."

"But your brand…?" she asked carefully. "It's very YA. Very clean."

"That's what pen names are for." He winked.

She laughed, covering her mouth. "Ohhh, we sneaky now."

Before he could respond, the office door clicked open. Mr. Burch appeared, nodding. Nia touched Tarrick's arm and whispered, "Good luck."

Tarrick stepped forward.

By the time he drove home, the sun was slipping low, bleeding orange behind the rows of palm trees. The city stretched wide around him—strip malls and murals, sirens in the distance, beauty and chaos stacked block by block.

Inside his car, the AC buzzed as he turned up La Brea, heading south.

He thought about the meeting. The way Mr. Burch raised an eyebrow at the synopsis. The surprise when Tarrick said the new book wouldn't be under his name, but the pseudonym *Marquis Kindrick*. The moment Burch read the title—**Sweat**—and smirked, just slightly.

It was done now. In motion. Tarrick had a real shot. The royalties from his last novel kept him stable, sure—but this? If it hit, it could change everything. A house in View Park-Windsor Hills overlooking the entire city maybe.

He should've been buzzing.

Instead, his mind wandered—to something else entirely.

"Whoever this heffa is that thinks she can sleep with my man?"

Shaunice's voice played in his head like a warning.

"She better be ready to get dealt with."

Tarrick gripped the wheel tighter.

They'd crossed a line. Just once. But once was enough.

The memory flared: Dante's breath on his neck. The weight of him. The way their bodies moved like they'd done it before. Tarrick had *tasted* him. Felt him. Let him in.

And then what?

He'd smiled and pitched a fake story to his publisher, all while hiding the real one pulsing in his blood.

I had my moment, Tarrick told himself. *It was heat. It was impulse. It's over.*

He needed to believe that. He needed to stop wanting more.

Because if Shaunice ever found out?

There wouldn't be a next chapter.

He turned down his street, the sunset throwing long shadows across cracked pavement. The world outside was cooling.

But inside, everything still burned.

CHAPTER FOURTEEN— *One More Day*

The light was already slicing through the blinds when Tarrick opened his eyes. His vision blurred with sleep, he turned his head and squinted at the wall. The calendar hung crooked. Marked-up squares, days crossed off. A quiet countdown.

Day six.

Just one more day until he'd have his place to himself again.
One day until temptation walked out the door.
One day until life could go back to normal.

Whatever normal was now.

He rolled onto his back and let out a breath.

But it hit him just as fast:
One more day in this tight-ass apartment.
One more day of awkward silences and guilty glances.
One more day pretending he didn't rewind the memory every time Dante walked past shirtless. Every time he said Tarrick's name in that voice.

"Can't he just do Lyft for the rest of the day?" Tarrick groaned to the ceiling. "Just stay gone."

Because every second Dante was still here was a risk.

A risk of something happening again.

A risk of getting used to it.

And then there was Shaunice.

One more day before her instincts kicked in. Before she noticed the shift. The silence. The sex she wasn't having. Before she followed the trail of tension back to him.

Tarrick swung his legs out of bed and rubbed the sleep from his face. The heat was already creeping in, but the forecast promised a cool-down—maybe even rain. A break was coming. The pressure would lift.

So would the guilt.

Or so he kept telling himself.

It was his sister's boyfriend. It could never happen again. It was a one-time mistake. He just had to make it to tomorrow.

Then he heard his name.

"Tarrick."

Dante's voice. From the living room.

Tarrick grabbed a pillow and pressed it in his face like he was dying a melodramatic death of suffocation, kicking his feet like a child. Then he sat up, smoothed his face, and stepped out like nothing had happened.

Dante was shirtless, standing by the window, handing him a small stack of mail. His basketball shorts sagged low. The bulge was obvious.

"You got mail," Dante said casually.

Tarrick barely looked at him. "Thanks." He turned toward his room, but Dante caught him by the arm.

"Wait."

Tarrick froze.

"You not gonna talk about it?" Dante asked.

Tarrick stayed neutral. "What's there to talk about?"

"I'm not gay," Dante said, his voice low, like it might crack if he said it too loud.

Tarrick raised an eyebrow. "Okay."

"I'm just saying—keep it quiet. Don't be telling nobody. Especially them queens downstairs—they look like they run their mouths."

Tarrick gave a dry laugh. "Wow. Really?"

Dante didn't answer.

Tarrick stepped in a little closer. "Had you done it before?"

Dante frowned. "What?"

"You know…" Tarrick's voice dropped. "Stuff with a guy. Not even in jail?"

Dante blinked.

"You needed to be taken care of somehow, right?" Tarrick asked.

Dante snapped back, "Just like when your sister stopped putting out and had me on the couch."

Tarrick's jaw ticked. Then: "But you liked it though. I wasn't just a hole. I saw your face. Heard your voice. You enjoyed every fucking second."

Dante's eyes narrowed. "You think that?"

Tarrick moved in, nearly touching. "I know that. And I think you want it again."

Dante didn't move.

"I'm with your sister," he said.

Tarrick smirked. "Didn't stop you before."

He kissed him.

Dante kissed back. Rough. Hungry. Like he'd been wanting more.

The mail slipped to the floor. Magazines scattered.

Tarrick dropped to his knees, tugged down Dante's shorts, and took him into his mouth like it was the only way to breathe.

Dante groaned. "Fuck… you really know how to work that mouth."

Tarrick looked up, tongue out, eyes wet, locked on him. Dante clenched his jaw.

"Suck it."

And Tarrick did. Deep. Slow. Wet.

What they didn't see:
AJ, outside, catching a glimpse through the cracked blind.

He gasped.

Fanned himself.

"Whew. It's hot out here," he whispered. "And hotter in there."

Then—Shaunice pulled into the lot.

Still in her scrubs. Talking to herself.

"Glad I got off early. Time to pack."

She grabbed her keys and headed up the stairs just as AJ came down—too fast, too sweaty.

"Shaunice! What you doing here?"

She frowned. "What you mean what I'm doing here? My brother lives here."

From the patio, José peeked, clearly entertained.

AJ forced a smile. "*Well,* you haven't been over to see me and José in a minute."

Shaunice raised an eyebrow. "*Well,* I'm starting to pack. We're moving back into our place tomorrow."

AJ wiped sweat from his brow.

"You okay?" she asked. "Why you sweating so hard?"

"We in the middle of a heatwave, girl," he said too quickly.

Shaunice's phone rang. She answered.

"Damn… I forgot to send that signature. I just got home… I really need to come back for that?"

Shaunice's face was pissed. AJ didn't know what was going on but his was relieved.

She turned around, heading back to her car. "I'll catch up with y'all later."

AJ exhaled like he'd been holding his breath for hours and hurried over to his patio where José had been watching. "You better tell me what you saw."

Upstairs, now in Tarrick's bedroom. Dante had Tarrick bent over the bed. Their naked bodies slick with sweat. The rhythm was primal.

The room was filled with moans, grunts, friction, need. Tarrick clutched the sheets, panting. "Harder… fuck… don't stop."

Dante's grip tightened. His thrusts grew deeper. It was heat. Hunger. Denial undone.

His breath caught.

Tarrick's body opened beneath him.

And with a final, broken groan, Dante came—deep, pulsing inside him.

Tarrick collapsed forward, chest heaving. And just like that, it happened again.

No excuses.
No pretending.
Just heat.

Just sweat.
Just one more day.

CHAPTER FIFTEEN— *Exhaustion*

The break room at the South L.A. Hospital was dim and stale, thick with the smell of burnt coffee and Lysol. Fluorescent lights buzzed overhead, and the vending machine in the corner whirred like it was thinking too hard. Shaunice sat slouched in a chair, scrubs wrinkled, her body heavy with something deeper than exhaustion.

A single tear slipped down her cheek. She didn't bother to wipe it.

"Girl," said a voice from the doorway. "What's wrong?"

Judy walked in holding a water bottle, her honey-brown curls pulled into a high puff. She wore the same scrubs as Shaunice—same color, same job—but somehow looked ten times fresher.

Shaunice let out a dry laugh, the kind that cracked in the middle. "What's right?"

Judy didn't press. She crossed the room and sat beside her, gently brushing the tear off Shaunice's face.

"They really made you come all the way back just to sign discharge paperwork?"

"Yeah," Shaunice said quietly. "But that ain't why I'm like this."

Judy raised an eyebrow. "Then what is it?"

Shaunice hesitated, staring down at her hands. The silence stretched until Judy leaned in, lowering her voice like she already knew the answer.

"Oh no. Don't tell me. Dante found out. About you and Dr. Greene?"

Shaunice shook her head. "No. It's still under wraps."

"Then what is it?"

"I don't know what to think." Shaunice's voice wavered. "He's never home now. Ever since he started driving for Lyft, he's always out. All hours. Says he's 'working.'"

Judy leaned back, lips pursed. "Didn't you push him to get a job, though?"

"I did," Shaunice admitted. "I've been on his ass for weeks about it. Now he's finally got income coming in, and I'm the one falling apart."

She rubbed her face with both hands, then sighed.

"What's eating me up is… he hasn't even noticed I'm not wearing my engagement ring."

Judy's eyes widened. "Wait, what? Where is it?"

Shaunice looked down. "At Terrell's place."

Judy blinked. "You left it at Dr. Greene's?"

Shaunice nodded, shame rolling off her like heat. "I took it off before we... you know. Didn't want that reminder while I was letting him have me."

She swallowed hard. "I knew exactly what I was doing. And I still did it."

"You are not the first nurse to fall for that man," Judy said, her voice gentler now. "Terrell's got that thing about him. That quiet, cocky energy. The way he talks to you like you're the only one in the room. You're not pathetic. You're human."

"I called him the next day," Shaunice said. "Told him I left my ring. He said he didn't see it. But I could hear it in his voice—he didn't even look. Just brushed me off."

"And Dante still hasn't noticed?"

"Not a damn word," Shaunice said. "It's been two days. That's what's messing with me the most. Like… does he even see me anymore?"

Judy rested a hand on her thigh. "So what are you gonna do?"

Shaunice didn't answer right away. She just looked straight ahead, her expression numb. "I don't know. I really don't."

At Tarrick's place, the mail was still scattered across the hardwood like a mess of unanswered questions. Tarrick knelt to pick it up—credit card offers, an envelope from DWP, and a thick one with his literary agent's return address. He thumbed through the stack with one hand, the other brushing his eye from a loose lash.

Behind him, the fridge opened and shut. Dante grabbed a bottle of water, the plastic crackling as he chugged it.

"I'm about to go get some rides in," Dante said.

"Before you head out," Tarrick said, turning toward him, "I got something."

Dante raised a brow.

"Four tickets to the advance screening of a new Lee Daniels film. At the theater by the Baldwin Hills - Crenshaw Mall. Real premiere— red carpet, cameras, all that. You and Shaun should roll with me."

Dante smiled. "That sounds dope."

But his expression shifted—just slightly. Something flickered in his eyes, quick as a shadow.

Tarrick noticed.

"You don't have to worry," he said. "Our secret's safe."

Dante didn't respond right away. He took another sip of water, eyes fixed on the floor.

"I'm not gonna say anything," Tarrick continued. "Trust me, I don't want the wrath of Shaunice either. But... we can't keep doing this."

He paused, letting the weight of the words settle.

"We got it out of our system. That was it."

Dante nodded slowly. "Yeah."

He turned to leave, but Tarrick called after him.

"Can I ask you something first?"

Dante stopped.

"Do you love my sister?"

Dante turned his head, eyes steady. "Yeah. That's why I proposed. Spent what I could on that ring."

He hesitated, then added, "But sometimes... I don't think she loves me the same. Not like she used to."

Tarrick looked at him for a long moment. "Then make sure she knows it. But don't be out here playing both sides."

Dante's jaw tightened.

"She's my sister," Tarrick went on. "You need to be faithful to her. No other women. Or men for that matter."

Dante looked him in the eyes. There was no anger in his face. Just something unreadable. Quiet. Dangerous.

"Then what do you call this?"

And with that, he walked out—leaving the door open behind him, and Tarrick standing in the thick silence with nothing but a fistful of mail and the memory of what they'd done.

CHAPTER SIXTEEN— *The Package*

The sun was setting slow over South L.A., gold bleeding into orange across the sky. On the patio outside AJ and José's unit, the tiki torches flickered as the grill hissed and popped with thick cuts of carne asada.

"Mmm, this food smells *so* damn good," AJ said, flipping a marinated slab with practiced flair.

José smirked, sipping white wine out of a stemless glass. "The food's not the only thing about to get grilled."

AJ raised an eyebrow.

"When Tarrick gets here," José said. "We need *all* the tea."

They both cackled.

Footsteps sounded on the stairs above, as they turned to him, instantly pretending to be casual.

Tarrick appeared, descending down the stairs from his apartment above in slow motion like a summer daydream—draped in a sleeveless, cream-colored knit set that hugged his chest and hit just above the knees. Skin moisturized, collarbone sharp. It wasn't loud, but it was *loud enough*.

"Okay, fashion," AJ murmured under his breath.

Before Tarrick could step onto the patio, a deep voice cut through the air.

"Excuse me."

They all turned.

A UPS driver was walking up the walkway, tall and fine and neatly pressed in his uniform. His skin was dark and glowing in the torchlight, arms strong, and the package in his hands big enough to make an impression.

"You Tarrick Daniels?"

"Yeah," Tarrick said, pausing.

"This package is for you."

Tarrick took it, a bit confused. "Thanks. I wasn't expecting anything. How'd you know it was me?"

The driver grinned. "I'm a fan of your books. Recognized you right away." Then, his eyes flicked down and back up—appreciative, but respectful. "You're lookin' good this evening, sir."

Tarrick smiled, caught off guard. "Appreciate that. And... I think you'll like my *new* book a lot."

"Oh yeah?" the driver said. "I'll keep an eye out. What's it called?"

Tarrick's stomach flipped. **Shit.** The book wasn't under his name. *Sweat* was by Marquis Kindrick. Not Tarrick Daniels.

Before he could stumble through a lie, the driver leaned in, smooth.

"You should give me your number. So I don't forget when it drops."

Tarrick hesitated only a second—then took his phone.

"Malcom" the UPS driver said introducing himself, as Tarrick finished typing in his number. "Looking forward to reading... and maybe seeing you again."

With a wink, he turned and walked off—package delivered.

From the patio, AJ exhaled dramatically. "Now *that* is what I call a large package."

Tarrick shook his head, laughing as he walked over with the large delivery. "Y'all don't miss a thing, do you?"

José glanced at AJ, then back at Tarrick. "Speaking of things not missed..."

Tarrick narrowed his eyes. "What?"

AJ grinned. "You first. What's in the package?"

"I don't know," Tarrick said, ripping the paper off. Inside, wrapped, was a large blown-up poster version of his book cover— *SWEAT*, bold in rainbow across the chest of a shirtless man with a man and woman behind him. His publisher's card sat on top: *Good luck and much success on the release.*

Tarrick pulled it out. The torchlight hit the glossy surface just right.

AJ whistled. "Okay, now *that's* a sexy cover."

José tilted his head. "Who's Marquis Kindrick?"

Tarrick hesitated. "It's a new pen name. This book's a little more... adult."

AJ's eyes lit up. "We love an alter ego. And don't worry, girl, our lips are sealed. Just like we covered for you earlier."

Tarrick froze. "What are you talking about?"

José sipped his wine.

AJ smirked. "Honey, you need to close them blinds tighter next time. I got a full show earlier. It was giving Skinemax after dark. If Shaunice had come up the stairs two minutes earlier—whew."

Tarrick's stomach dropped. "AJ, no…"

"Relax," AJ said. "I didn't say anything."

José chimed in, tone sly. "But let's be real. Was it a one-time thing? Or is Dante the inspiration for this book?"

Tarrick shot him a look. "Y'all need to stop."

"I'm just saying," José said, raising his glass. "If *I* had a man like that up in my sheets—"

"Seriously," Tarrick cut in.

"Yeah, what am I?" AJ shoots at José.

Tarrick stressed. "Shaunice can't know. If she finds out, it's over. Like... our relationship as siblings? Done. I might even end up missing."

They went quiet. The flames flickered. The weight of it settled in.

AJ finally spoke. "We got you. But you better figure out what you're doing. Secrets sweat through walls, girl."

Across the city—

Judy sat at the nurses' station, her eyes on her screen. Dr. Terrell Greene's hospital profile glowed under the harsh overhead lights. His headshot was clean-cut, smiling just enough. God, he looked good.

"No wonder everybody wants a piece," she muttered.

She stood, tossing her stethoscope over her neck, and made her way to his office at the very end of the hall. The hallway was quiet—end-of-shift energy. She knocked once, didn't hear anything, then pushed the door open.

And froze.

Terrell was behind his desk—but not sitting. He was standing—**balls-deep** in a woman bent over the filing cabinet. Pants at his ankles. Sweat glistening on his back. His hips moved in slow, unbothered strokes, like he had all the time in the world.

The woman gasped, her top halfway off, breasts swinging with each thrust. "Oh my God, you forgot to lock—"

Terrell turned just enough to register Judy. His thick, slick dick slid out, pointing at her, as if confirming she was next.

Judy blinked, then stepped back.

"Sorry," she said, calmly. "Didn't know you had an after-hours appointment."

She pulled the door closed behind her and walked away, her pulse racing. A smile tugged at the corner of her mouth—but she wasn't ready to unpack that yet.

CHAPTER SEVENTEEN — *See Something You Like?*

Tarrick woke up with a jolt, eyes darting to the calendar on the wall.

Day Seven. Finally.

In the voice of comedian Martin Lawrence from his hit sitcom, Tarrick muttered, "Get to steppin,'" with a half-smile, dragging himself out of bed.

He opened the bedroom door to silence. No pots clanging, no music blasting from Shaunice's phone, no Dante singing off-key. The living room was still. Their bags were gone. So were they.

"Hello?" he called. Nothing.

He padded down the hall, peeked into the spare room. Empty. Clean. Quiet.

They were gone.

Meanwhile, beneath palm trees swaying and waves rolling in with steady rhythm, Shaunice and Dante walked side by side along the shoreline. The beach was alive, sun low and gold, bathing the sand in heat.

Dante had ditched his shirt and let the breeze hit his chest. But it wasn't about the weather today—it was about space. And peace.

"So, what did you wanna talk about?" Shaunice asked, voice light but careful.

Dante nodded. "I just… I don't know. I've been thinking. We been through a lot. All the tension, the moving, the back and forth… I just want today to be chill. Before we take our stuff back into our apartment."

She nodded slowly. "I can do that."

"I been making decent money with Lyft," he added. "And I got a callback for that maintenance gig downtown. So things are moving."

Shaunice smiled, but it didn't reach all the way. "That's good. Real good."

Dante looked over. "You sure? You seem… I don't know."

"I've just had a lot on my mind."

"Like what?"

She hesitated. Like the fact I took my ring off to sleep with a doctor? Like the fact I think you might be cheating too?
None of that came out.

Instead, she shrugged, her hand stuffed in her pocket to conceal. "Just tired. But yeah… excited to move back into the apartment today."

Just then, a shadow cut across the sand in front of them. She caught the scent of saltwater and cologne before she saw him.

Shaunice looked up—and nearly stopped walking.

Dr. Terrell Greene was coming toward them, shirtless and glistening in board shorts, fresh from the ocean. His chest caught the light just right. His abs moved when he walked, and so did Shaunice's gaze.

Dante noticed. He noticed everything.

"See something you like?" he asked.

Shaunice snapped out of it.

Beside Terrell, in a bold emerald bikini that left little to the imagination, was Judy—cool as ever, curves out, sunglasses perched like armor. She acted like this moment wasn't messy at all.

Terrell smiled wide. "Shaunice. Hey, look at that—South Bay got even better today. This your man?"

"Yeah," she said tightly. "This is Dante."

Terrell reached out. "Nice to meet you, man."

Dante shook his hand—reluctantly.

Shaunice exchanged a glance with Judy, but Judy just adjusted her sunglasses and smiled like she was on vacation.

"Well," Terrell said, voice low and smooth. "I'll see you around the office Shaun."

Shaunice nodded, lips tight. "Yeah. Sure."

She turned to watch him walk away—every muscle in his back flexing in motion, his shorts clinging to him like intention. Judy beside him, strutting like they hadn't just been caught in high-definition.

Shaunice blinked hard, turned to Dante, who was already watching her. She gave a thin smile.

She watched a whole-ass doctor walk away... while standing next to a man still chasing a maybe-job. What the hell was she doing?

She didn't say it out loud. But it rang loud in her head.

CHAPTER EIGHTEEN — *Still Warm*

Tarrick sat at his desk, bouncing one knee. The oversized thick poster of *SWEAT* lay sprawled across his bed behind him—bold, slick, and fully alive in print. The glossy cover practically shimmered in the light, the shirtless model daring anyone to look away.

He glanced at his phone's contact list.

Malcolm.

The UPS driver. Broad, confident, respectful with a grin that knew what it was doing.

Tarrick tapped on the name, then tapped out a message:
Hey. It's Tarrick.

He hit send. Simple. Clean.

For once, he was texting a man who wasn't off-limits. Not his sister's fiancé. Not a secret.

It felt… healthy. And maybe even hopeful.

Before he could overthink it, his phone rang.

"Hey," he answered.

His agent's voice was electric. "Sweat is going to print! It's official—we're launching under Marquis Kindrick. Big push from the distributor. I mean, this thing has legs."

Tarrick blinked. "What? Seriously?"

"All systems go. Now we just need to talk about rollout—how to market this since it's not under you and your YA base, but we'll handle it. Congrats, for real."

He stared at the poster again. The book. The moment. The future he was finally claiming.

"Thank you," he whispered, letting the words settle in his chest.

On the other side of town, under a cloudless sky and the sharp coastal air of Manhattan Beach, Shaunice rang the doorbell of a sleek glass house that looked more like a sculpture than a home.

The door opened.

Terrell stood in nothing but a robe, abs gleaming, smile cocky.

"You ever wear real clothes?" Shaunice asked, brushing past him without waiting for an invite.

He didn't stop her. "Welcome back."

"I left my engagement ring here," she said. "I need to find it."

Up the floating staircase she went, scanning like she was searching for more than just jewelry. Guilt. Closure. Control.

The master bedroom was enormous—polished floors, floor-to-ceiling windows, and furniture that looked untouched. But what stopped her wasn't the decor.

It was Judy.

Sitting at the edge of the bed in a cropped tee and lace underwear. Hair slicked back, face unreadable.

The moment stretched.

Shaunice let out a dry laugh. "Wow."

Judy smirked but didn't move.

Shaunice went to the bed and started flipping pillows, pulling back sheets, yanking open drawers like she was on a mission. Which she was.

Terrell appeared in the doorway, leaning against the frame like a man watching a show.

"You sure I didn't blow it straight into another dimension?" he asked.

Shaunice shot him a glare. "Don't."

"You were loud," he said. "Could've echoed in the walls."

"You don't get to play games like that at the beach. Not in front of Dante. He's about to be my husband."

"All he did was say hi," Judy chimed in, voice silk-wrapped in steel.

Shaunice turned on her. "And you… wasted no time, huh?"

Judy tilted her head. "Look at him. He's sexy as fuck."
Then, quieter: "So are you."

That stopped Shaunice in her tracks. The drawer in her hand slipped closed.

Terrell walked to the bed, untied the belt of his robe, and let it fall.

Shaunice didn't mean to look—but she did. She always did.

He was thick. Hanging heavy. Already half-hard. A man who knew what his body did to people.

Judy slid off the bed, unhooking her bra as she walked past him.

Terrell sat, voice low and coaxing on his bed. "You said she looked good, right?"

He looked at Judy.

"Show her how good."

Judy turned to Shaunice. No smirk now. Just hunger.

Shaunice froze.

"What are you doing?" she asked, heart knocking against her ribs.

Judy looked at Terrell, waiting. His nod came slow and certain.

Judy leaned in and kissed her.

Soft. Deliberate.

Shaunice didn't move.

She didn't stop it either.

The second kiss came slower, lips grazing, heat building. Beneath them, Terrell exhaled. The bed creaked as he adjusted, arousal unmistakable.

Shaunice knew exactly what she was doing now. So did Judy.

This wasn't about love. It wasn't even about lust. It was about escape and performance—from guilt, from boredom, from herself, and performance for Dr. Terrell Greene.

Terrell laid back as the women leaned over him, their lips softly finding each other, and he had front row seats.

They were doing it for him. For attention. For control. For something they couldn't name.

But no one said stop.

Shaunice's fingers suddenly brushed her engagement ring under a sheet, she couldn't believe she found it.

Still warm.

Still hers.

But suddenly, it felt like a lie.

In the morning, they'd all pretend nothing happened. But the sheets would still smell like guilt.

CHAPTER NINETEEN — *Just Me*

It had been a week since the apartment emptied out.

No more damp towels slung over chairs. No more Shaunice storming from room to room on her phone. No more Dante lounging shirtless on the couch like a man who owned the place.

Just silence.

Tarrick stood in front of the mirror, buttoning his shirt beneath a charcoal-gray suit jacket that had waited too long for a reason. The apartment felt bigger now. Lonelier, maybe. But quieter. And sometimes quiet was what you needed to hear yourself think.

The rain had finally come—late, like everything in this damn city. It beat gently against the windowpane now, washing away the last of the suffocating heat that had lingered like a fever.

Bad weather for a movie premiere.

Tarrick adjusted his collar, smoothing the lapels. Tonight was the big night. Lee Daniels' new film was premiering in the theater at Baldwin Hills-Crenshaw—one of those red-carpet events with velvet ropes, flashing cameras, and L.A. trying to act like it wasn't built on broken dreams.

He had four tickets.

Shaunice and Dante were going. Of course they were.

And the fourth?

Tarrick smiled to himself, just a little.

Malcolm.

They'd texted here and there all week—nothing too serious. But tonight would be the first time they'd be out together. A real date. A public one. Tarrick wasn't sure what that meant, but it felt like something.

A knock at the front door broke his thoughts. Sharp and sure.

He grabbed his phone, and crossed the apartment.

The rain was still coming down, steady and silver, when he opened the front door.

Malcolm stood there in a black turtleneck and a tailored coat, umbrella in hand, smile as calm as ever.

"This should keep us dry," Malcolm said, raising it up with a slight grin.

Tarrick laughed, stepping forward into the doorway—into something new that smelt damn good.

The lobby of the Baldwin Hills theater was alive with movement —umbrellas collapsing, heels clicking across tile, velvet ropes herding the Black glitterati of South L.A. Gowns shimmered. Suits gleamed. The red carpet, usually rolled out under bright sun and cell phones, had been pulled indoors tonight to escape the storm.

Tarrick and Malcolm stepped into the warmth of it all, shaking off the chill.

And then—because of course—AJ appeared, headset on, clipboard in hand, wearing a laminated STAFF badge like it was couture.

"Well, well, well," AJ sang, stopping them with one hand on his hip. "If it isn't Mr. Daniels, not Lee. The red carpet is right this way, sir."

Tarrick laughed. "You working this?"

"Somebody's gotta keep this show cute and on time," AJ said. "And I even got José in. VIP. Section B."

"I'll make sure to say hi if I bump into him."

"You better," AJ said, glancing at Malcolm with quick approval. "You brought a date and didn't tell me?"

"This is Malcolm," Tarrick said, introducing him.

"Pleasure," Malcolm offered, smiling.

"Mm-hmm," AJ said, already clocking everything. "Red carpet, baby. Don't make me drag you to it."

Tarrick shook his head. "I think we'll skip it tonight."

AJ leaned in dramatically. "Oop, is Marquis shy?"

"Marquis isn't here," Tarrick said, smoothing his jacket. "Tonight it's just me."

AJ winked. "You're lucky you fine."

He disappeared into the crowd like mist in heels. Passing a tall glass sculpture, custom made for the movie by the bar.

Malcolm leaned close. "That was AJ?"

Tarrick nodded. "Yeah. A whole character."

"I like him."

"You would."

They moved toward the theater doors, passing a photo booth as Tarrick glanced around, then pulled out his phone. Still no sign of Shaunice or Dante.

He sent a quick text:
Y'all close?

The response came immediately.
On the way.

Tarrick showed it to Malcolm. "Late. Typical."

Malcolm laughed. "You know Black people ain't ever on time."

Tarrick raised an eyebrow. "You saying we?"

"I mean… I'm punctual adjacent."

They both laughed, and something softened between them—ease settling into the moment.

Malcolm looked around. "Think we'll see any real celebrities tonight?"

"Mo'Nique should be here," Tarrick said. "Friends of the director — folks tend to show up."

Malcolm's eyes lit up. "You come to stuff like this a lot?"

"I get invited from time to time. Doesn't always mean I go."

Malcolm looked at him, warm. "Glad you did tonight."

Tarrick met his gaze. There was a pause. A shift.

And then the theater lights flickered—showtime approaching.

Tarrick turned toward the entrance just as the doors swung open.

In walked Shaunice and Dante.

Shaunice, radiant in a black velvet gown. Dante in a forest green suit, sharp lines and unreadable eyes. Her hand looped casually through his arm.

Tarrick tensed just slightly.

Malcolm noticed. "That them?"

"Yeah," Tarrick said, clearing his throat. "That's them."

And just like that, the calm was over.

CHAPTER TWENTY— *Popcorn & Glass*

The film was minutes from starting, but Shaunice needed a drink.

The buzz of the theater lobby swirled behind her as she slid onto a barstool, velvet gown hugging her figure. She flagged down the bartender. "Shot of tequila."

Before the glass even hit the counter, a voice slid in beside her.

"Fancy seeing you here."

Shaunice turned.

Judy, draped in gold silk and looking far too comfortable, smiled as she sipped her cocktail.

Shaunice blinked. "Judy. Wow. You clean up."

"I do what I can," Judy said, then leaned in. "Terrell invited me."

Shaunice stiffened slightly. "Did he?"

Before Judy could respond, Terrell approached from behind, all swagger and cologne.

"Hello, ladies," he said smoothly, eyes flicking to Shaunice's waist, then lower.

"You should sit with us," Judy said, her hand brushing his arm. "That seat next to me's still open. And who knows, maybe you swing by our place after?"

Shaunice rolled her eyes and held up her left hand.

"I'm very much engaged," she said coolly—then added, almost as an afterthought, "Happily."

Terrell smirked. "Come on, baby, don't be like that." He reached out, tugging playfully at her arm like it was still a game between them.

Shaunice snapped her arm back. "Don't."

"Hey!"

The voice boomed across the lobby.

Dante.

He was already charging forward, suit jacket flaring behind him, eyes locked on Terrell. Before anyone could react—

CRACK.

Dante's fist connected with Terrell's jaw. The sound cut through the chatter like a record scratch. Gasps rippled through the crowd.

"Keep your hands off my woman!" Dante barked.

Judy dropped to the floor beside Terrell, who was now holding his face. "Are you okay?"

"I'm good," Terrell muttered. Then he lunged—slamming Dante into the large glass sculpture that shattered upon impact as the crowd shrieked and scrambled out of the way.

Chaos.
Popcorn scattered. Stilettos backed up. Ushers froze.

Tarrick rushed in, heart pounding. "Oh my God—"

AJ and José appeared out of nowhere, eyes wide with curiosity and phones halfway raised.

"Don't do it," Tarrick snapped at them. "Not tonight."

Dante and Terrell wrestled near a poster stand.

"Stop it!" Shaunice shouted. "Both of you!"

Judy yelled for someone to intervene. Ushers tried to pull them apart. Finally, the two men were separated, breathing hard, glaring.

Dante's voice cracked with fury. "Don't you ever disrespect my fiancée again."

Terrell's lip bled slightly as he wiped it with the back of his hand. Then, calm as ever, he delivered the knife:

"Your fiancée disrespected you the second she took my dick."

Silence.

It rippled through the crowd like static.

AJ and José froze, eyes darting between Dante and Shaunice. Tarrick felt his stomach cave in.

Malcolm, just steps away, said nothing—but his face said everything.

Shaunice's mouth opened. She stared at Dante. "I—I'm sorry."

Dante looked gutted. "So it's true."

It wasn't just Terrell's mouth.

The air had changed. All eyes were on her now.

Shaunice stood taller, defensive and shaking. "Well—you're no saint either. I know you've been messing around too. So don't act like you're some victim."

Tarrick's spine stiffened.

How much did she know?

AJ and José glanced at Tarrick.

Tarrick couldn't meet their eyes. He looked at Dante instead. Dante's face was unreadable before turning back to Shaunice.

"Come on," Dante said, low. "We need to talk. In private. Not like this."

Shaunice hesitated, but followed.

AJ turned to the crowd. "Alright y'all, show's over. Let's keep it pushin'. Movie's starting. Go ahead find your seats."

One guest muttered, "The real movie's out here."

José clapped once, sharp. "Back to the movie drama, please."

The crowd slowly broke apart. But something else had shattered.

Something you couldn't sweep off a theater floor.

Tarrick felt every crack of it.

CHAPTER TWENTY-ONE — *The Lie We Chose*

Tarrick stood outside a private meeting room, heart pounding.

Voices echoed through the door—muffled, heated, too loud for a room meant for reconciliation.

Shaunice. Dante.

This was it. Everything that had been simmering behind glances and silence was about to explode.

He took a breath. Held it.

"—so who is it?" Shaunice's voice rang out, sharp and demanding.

Tarrick froze.

Dante fired back, his voice rough. "No. Don't try to flip this. You slept with Terrell Greene. That freak from the hospital?"

A beat of silence.

Then Shaunice, quiet: "I'm so sorry."

Tarrick's chest ached. He leaned closer to the door.

"How long?" Dante asked.

"A couple weeks," she said, barely audible.

Tarrick shut his eyes.

God. It's all unraveling.

And then—Shaunice again. "So what about you? Do I know her?"

Tarrick held his breath.

Boy, do you ever, he thought.

Footsteps approached.

He turned to see Malcolm, dressed sharp but concerned.

"You alright?" Malcolm asked, keeping his voice low.

Tarrick nodded, barely. "I need to be in there with them. I'll be right out, okay?"

Malcolm gave a gentle nod as Tarrick pushed open the door.

Shaunice looked up. Her voice cracked with bitterness. "Perfect timing. Dante was just about to tell me who he's been sleeping with."

Tarrick hesitated. He and Dante locked eyes.

A long, electric pause.

So much unsaid in a single stare.

Then Dante broke it.

"You don't know *her*," he said, turning to Shaunice.

Tarrick let out a quiet breath he didn't know he'd been holding.

Shaunice wasn't having it. "You don't know that. What's her name?"

Dante blinked once. "Pam. From Long Beach."

He looked at the floor. "I'm sorry."

Shaunice stepped back like the floor moved beneath her. "Jesus. What are we doing? Do we even want to get married?"

Dante didn't answer at first.

Then, flat: "I'm starting to question that myself."

Shaunice stared at him, then at Tarrick, then stormed past them both and out the door—heels sharp, breath ragged.

Tarrick moved to follow, but paused beside Dante.

He leaned in.

"Thank you," Tarrick said quietly.

Dante didn't look at him. "I didn't do it for you," he muttered. "I just… can't have people knowing I slept with a guy."

Tarrick nodded. "I'm not saying anything. We're the only ones that know."

"I know."

Dante paused. Then finally: "It'll be our secret."

They looked at each other again. For a second, it felt like a question was hanging between them.

Maybe Dante wanted something to seal the silence.

Once, Tarrick might've let him. Might've blurred that line all over again.

But not tonight.

Not anymore.

He took a step back.

He had something real waiting for him. Something that didn't need hiding.

Tarrick turned and left Dante standing alone.

In the lobby, Malcolm looked up as Tarrick approached.

"You good?" he asked, gentle.

Tarrick adjusted his coat, gave a quiet smile. "Yeah. Sorry for keeping you waiting."

Malcolm opened the door, umbrella in hand.

"Let's go."

And together, they stepped back into the rain.

CHAPTER TWENTY-TWO — *Thicker Than Sweat*

ONE MONTH LATER…

Tarrick lay sprawled across his bed in his now-quiet apartment, robe open in just his tight black briefs, face lit by the TV glow. For once, the drama wasn't his—it was *Beyond the Gates*, his favorite daytime soap opera, and the Duprees were giving everything, along with his favorite villainess, Dana/Leslie/Ana, or whatever her new alias was that week. He cackled, throwing popcorn in his mouth and living for the mess.

He could breathe.

No more tension. No more secrets sitting across from him at dinner. Just him, his space, and his own soundtrack playing as loud as he wanted. He could cook without someone stealing the last of the eggs. He could dance around naked—which he did. Often.

And he could have company again.

Which he definitely did.

Malcolm was over nearly every night now.

The man was all three C's: **caring, charming, charismatic**. He didn't have to try. He just opened the door, and that smile? That smile could make Tarrick leak before anything else even happened.

The way Malcolm moved on him—kisses up his neck to that exact spot. The way he'd eat him out on the couch. The way they'd fuck in the kitchen, the shower, against the front door. No one to interrupt. No one to whisper stop.

They got so loud once, the neighbor banged the ceiling with a broom. They laughed.

Kept going.

It was perfect.

The book had dropped, too.

SWEAT. Nationwide. Under *Marquis Kindrick*.

No one knew it was his story or how true it was. Just how he wanted it. The secrets remained buried in those pages.

One afternoon, he walked into the local bookstore on Crenshaw. There it was—front table. Bold. Bare-chested. Honest. Just in time for the Pride Month display table.

He stood staring at it until a voice called behind him.

Shaunice, holding two iced caramel macchiatos.

She didn't know.

And she never would.

Because their bond mattered more than any release party or literary brag. Because some secrets didn't belong in the light. And because blood—no matter how messy—was still thicker than sweat.

She passed the display table without looking twice. He didn't flinch.

They sipped their drinks together as a man strolled past—tall, bald, chocolate, Boris Kodjoe fine.

They both watched.

Shaunice raised an eyebrow. "Gay or straight?"

Tarrick sipped. "Bi and confusing."

She laughed. "If he's anything but unavailable, I'm ready."

No engagement ring. No Dante. No Terrell. Just a woman re-learning her worth.

And a brother beside her, finally at peace.

AUTHOR'S NOTE— *Marquis Kindrick*

Some stories write themselves.
Some stories burn holes through you until you let them out.

This one did both.

I wrote Sweat in the middle of a real heatwave—sweat on my neck, sweat on my conscience. I told myself it was fiction. I told myself it didn't matter. But every scene I typed came from somewhere I'd lived, or somewhere I wanted to.

Call it therapy. Call it sin. Call it storytelling.

But know this—every page carries truth.

Even if I never say whose.

—MK